SPACE CASE

by Edward Marshall · pictures by James Marshall

PUFFIN BOOKS

It came from outer space

to have a look around

and to meet the natives,

who were not especially friendly.

Really! Everyone seemed so uncooperative.
The thing from outer space was beginning to lose heart.

But at the corner of Maple and Elm

some interesting folks appeared.

"Wow!" said Buddy McGee. "Will you look at *that*!"
"What a great costume!" said Lily.
"It must be that new kid from down the block,"
  said Mary Louise.
"Come with us," said Buddy.

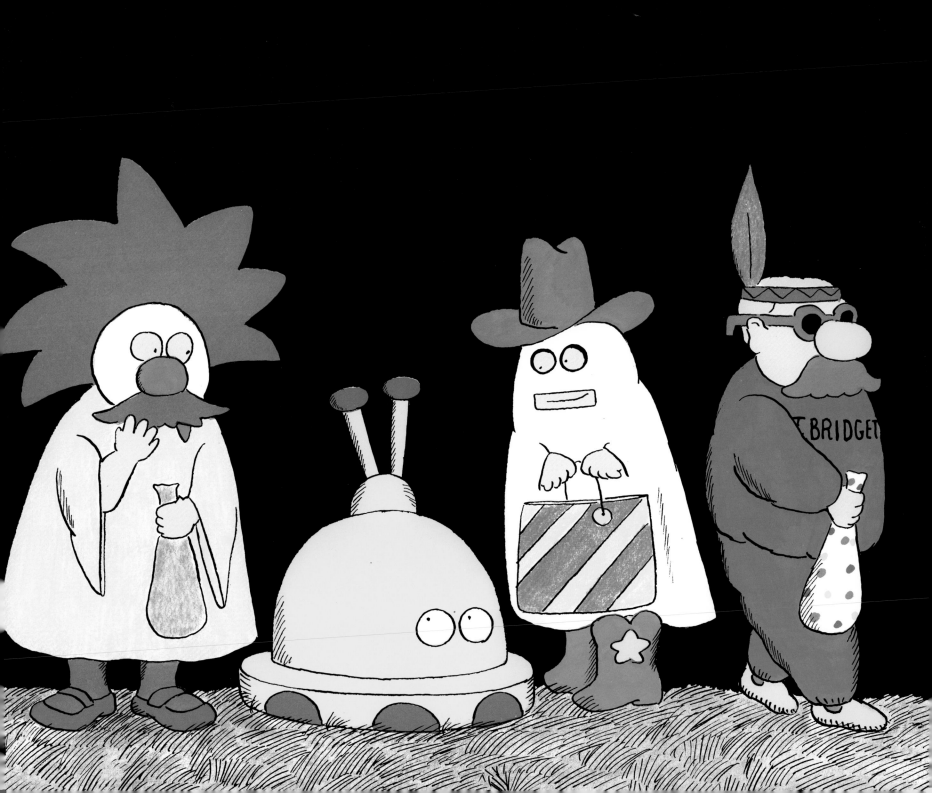

"Trick or treat!" shouted Buddy.

And a nice lady gave them all treats.

Soon the thing was having a fine time.

Trick-or-treating was lots of fun!

When their bags were full of goodies, the kids stopped
at the schoolyard to stuff themselves silly.
"Trick or treat!" beeped the thing.
"There's something weird about that new kid,"
whispered Lily.

Heading home, Buddy noticed he was being followed.
For the first time he took a good look at the thing.
"*You're* not the kid from down the block," said Buddy.
"Trick or treat!" beeped the thing.
"Do you want to spend the night at my house?"
asked Buddy.

Mr. McGee let them in.

"You'll like my room," said Buddy.

After studying the dictionary, the thing found it easier to communicate.

"The location of my origin is in outer space," it beeped.

"I thought so," said Buddy. "We'll have lots to talk about in the morning."

When Buddy turned out the lights, the thing turned out *its* lights and lowered its antennae.

Mrs. McGee was surprised to see the thing at the breakfast table.

"What on earth is *that*?" she said.

"It's from outer space," said Buddy.

"Yes, dear," said his mother.

While Buddy ate his fried eggs, the thing atomized a glass of orange juice.

"Fantastic toys these kids have," said Mr. McGee.

"Are you *sure* you want to come to school?"
 asked Buddy.
"Unquestionably," beeped the thing.
"I want to observe."

Everyone was too excited by Mr. Jones's reptiles to notice the thing.

"Good heavens!" beeped the thing.
"What peculiar-looking specimens."

"And now," said Mr. Jones, putting away his reptiles, "it's time for your space projects."

"Uh-oh," said Buddy. "I forgot to do mine!"

"Calm down," beeped the thing.

The first project was a homemade rocket.
"How primitive," beeped the thing.

John Watson showed a model of Mars.
"All wrong," beeped the thing.

"And what do *you* have to show us, Buddy?"
asked Mr. Jones.
Before Buddy could reply, the thing proceeded to the
front of the class and did some fancy mathematics at
the blackboard.
"Er," said Buddy, "that's my robot."
"Very clever indeed," said Mr. Jones. "That's worth an
A minus."
"Whew!" said Buddy.

"School was fun," beeped the thing. "But I wouldn't want
  to do it every day. When do we go trick-or-treating?"
"But that's only once a year," said Buddy.
"Oh," beeped the thing. "I just remembered an appointment
  on Jupiter."
"Wait!" cried Buddy.
  And he explained all about Christmas.
"Why, that's only two zyglots away," beeped the thing.
"I think I'll come back for that!"
  It started to pick up speed…

and in a flash it was gone.
"Wow!" said Buddy.